Sue Carabine

Illustrations by

Shauna Mooney Kawasaki

GIBBS SMITH

TO ENRICH AND INSPIRE HUMANKIND

16 15 14 13   14 13 12 11

Text and illustrations © 2003 Gibbs Smith, Publisher

Published by
Gibbs Smith
P.O. Box 667
Layton, Utah 84041

1.800.835.4993 orders
www.gibbs-smith.com

Designed and produced by TTA Design
Printed and bound in China
Gibbs Smith books are printed on either recycled, 100% post-consumer waste, FSC-certified papers or on paper produced from a 100% certified sustainable forest/controlled wood source.

ISBN 13: 978-1-58685-269-6
ISBN 10: 1-58685-269-8

'Twas the night before Christmas
at the town's fire station,
Where brave firefighters
were gathering donations.

The same thing was happening
in towns coast to coast,
Firefighters were doing
the thing they loved most:

Helping out kids and folks
who needed assistance,
And answering their calls,
regardless of distance.

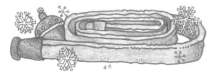

At Christmastime, most of
the treasures they sought
Were gifts for the children,
which many folks brought.

And as they worked hard
on this night of all nights,
The Governor rang up and said,
"Something's not right.

"A sleigh has been spotted
with deer all around,
There's no one to drive them.
St. Nick can't be found!"

Said the captain, "Don't panic.

This must be a first:

It seems we've lost Santa.

Now, what could be worse!

"Christmas Eve is upon us,
we have to act fast
To make sure this Christmas
will not be our last!"

The firefighters decided
the kids should not know
That Old Santa was missing,
'twould be too hard a blow!

They dashed to their engines
with all their gear on,
The sirens were wailing
as the trucks rushed along.

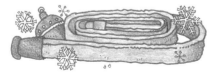

It was tough moving fast
at this time of the day.
Though traffic was heavy,
it moved out of their way.

Seems like the town folks
knew that something was wrong,
So they all did their best
to help move things along.

The firefighters arrived
at the scene, looked around,
Took hold of the bridles
to calm the deer down.

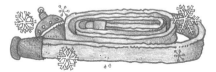

One noticed large footprints
pressed deep in the snow,
So several were chosen
who were willing to go

And follow the tracks.

Moving slowly, precise,

They trailed the signs closely,

sometimes checking twice.

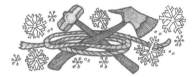

The prints led to the roof
of a very tall house,
And they gingerly followed
as quiet as a mouse.

At the sooty brick chimney,

the footsteps had stopped,

The firefighters gazed down

through the flue—a long drop.

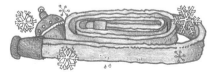

They saw something moving,
could hear a strange sound,
Then knew right away that
St. Nick had been found!

They heard him call softly,
"Is somebody there?
It's cold and it's dark,
and there's no room to spare!"

"We're here," called the captain,
"Nick, are you okay?"
"I'm fine, but I'm stuck!
I can't move either way!

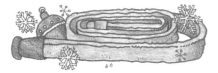

"It must be the pudding
dear Mrs. Claus fixed;
I ate every bite
to the very last licks.

"But please get me out,"
each heard Santa sigh,
"I know my poor reindeer
are ready to fly!"

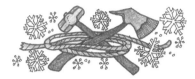

"Now don't worry, Santa,
you'll be out in a jiff.
Guys, get hooks and ladders!
They'll give him a lift."

So the firefighters pitched in,
like these crews always do,
Got a rope around Santa
to pull him up through.

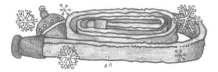

They shoved and they hoisted
and everyone tugged,
But dear old St. Nicholas
just couldn't be budged.

Pretty soon the old gent
was beginning to doubt
That these hardy firefighters
could help him get out.

"I've got an idea,"
one bystander declared.
"We used it in training
to free a trapped mare.

"This slippery soap should
take care of these troubles."
And before Santa knew it,
he was covered in bubbles!

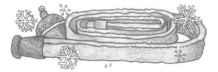

He was pushed from the bottom
and pulled from the top
Until at one point
St. Nick thought he would pop.

Then a brave firefighter
slowly let himself down
To stand on Nick's shoulders,
which brought forth a frown.

"What you doin', young fella,
yer foot's in my mouth!
Are you plannin' on stompin'
until I go south?"

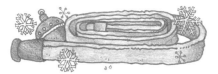

"Grab hold of my ankles,"
the young man replied.
"Now, that's hard to do, son,
with arms pinned to my side."

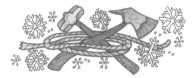

Then, a trusty old firefighter
arrived on the scene,
Had whiskers like Santa's,
but was lanky and lean.

He took out a huge axe
(which made everyone gasp),
Said, "I'll fix this problem
with one well-placed bash!"

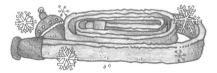

A nervous St. Nick called,
"You're gonna use that?
Hold on there, old timer,
let's first have a chat!"

"Since nothing else works, Nick,
let's give this a try.
You'll be free as a bird
in the wink of an eye!"

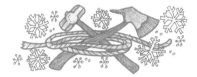

He heaved it o'erhead,
was about to let go,
When he heard a small voice
calling up from below.

"Oh, please don't hurt Santa,"
the little voice piped,
"There's a much safer way
that I know you will like!"

Up the tall chimney
where Santa was parked,
Eight-year-old Suzie
called into the dark,

"My daddy's a fireman,
my hero! You see,
He taught me so much
as I sat on his knee.

"Sometimes the tough things
just aren't hard at all,
And I think I can help
though I know I'm quite small.

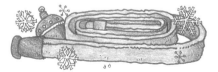

"St. Nick, if you hear me
above all this noise,
Let go of your sack
'cause it's chock full of toys!"

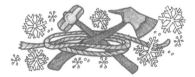

"That idea sounds worthwhile,
I'll give it a try,
I'll do anything to bid
this black chimney goodbye."

Though his cramped hands felt numb
and his belly was sore,
Nick slowly released
the large sack with its store.

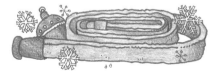

Well, joy of all joys,
he could feel lots more space!
So he crept down the chimney
(with no time to waste).

While everyone cheered,
Santa Claus touched the ground,
And was greeted by firefighters,
who rallied around.

"You were daring, my friends,
thanks for helping me out;
And, Dad, you taught Suzie
what caring's about!

"Now it's late, so I'm asking
you firefighters worldwide,
To help me spread cheer
on this Christmas Eve night!"

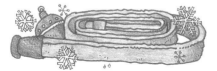

And that's how it happened—
the best Christmas ever
'Cause everyone worked hard
and shared fun together!

Then Nick called, "Brave firefighters,
it's been a great night,
May the glow in your skies
come from sparkling Yule lights!"